THE NEW BABY
BY MERCER MAYER

A Random House PICTUREBACK® Book

Random House 🏠 **New York**

The New Baby book, characters, text, and images © 1983 Mercer Mayer. LITTLE CRITTER, MERCER MAYER'S LITTLE CRITTER, and MERCER MAYER'S LITTLE CRITTER and Logo are registered trademarks of Orchard House Licensing Company. All rights reserved. Published in the United States by Random House Children's Books, a division of Random House, Inc., New York. Originally published in 1983 by Golden Books Publishing Company, Inc. PICTUREBACK, RANDOM HOUSE, and the Random House colophon are registered trademarks of Random House, Inc.
www.randomhouse.com/kids
Educators and librarians, for a variety of teaching tools, visit us at
www.randomhouse.com/teachers
Library of Congress Control Number: 82-84111
ISBN-13: 978-0-307-11942-1   ISBN-10: 0-307-11942-4
Printed in the United States of America
24 23 22 21 20 19 18 17
First Random House Edition 2006

Dad said, "We have a new baby and she's coming home today."

I got out my ball and bat
and all my favorite games
to show to the baby.

I found my favorite picture book
and read it out loud to the baby.

But the new baby didn't
pay any attention to me.

She cried a lot…
even when I told
her my best joke.

I made my funniest
face ever and she
cried even louder.

I tried to dress her
but she was too
wiggly and floppy.

And sometimes
she smelled funny
and Mom had
to change her.

So what can you do
with a new baby?

Mom says we can cuddle her…

...and rock her to sleep.

We can tickle her tummy
and make her laugh…

...or give her a rattle
to play with.

I can give her my finger to grab…

...and let her pull my nose.

I can take her for a walk
and show her to my friends.

They think I'm so lucky.